MIKE YOUN

GH00870004

SUPERTED

AND THE BLUE WHALES

Illustrations by
Rob Lee and David Blake

Muller, Blond & White

Not long ago, a small girl was playing in a sandy bay somewhere in Wales. The tide was out and she wandered from one rock-pool to another, searching for tiny fish and shrimps.

Soon she found herself in the shadow of something large and dark blue-grey. At first she thought it was a wall of rock, but when she reached out her hand to touch it, it felt smooth and soft.

Suddenly, she stepped back and screamed. In front of her was the biggest whale she had ever seen!

Meanwhile, in a space station thousands of miles away, SuperTed's strange friend from the planet Spot was taking a bath.

"Eoowoom . . . splash! splash!" he shouted as he played with his toy submarine. Suddenly, his game was interrupted by the sound of an alarm, and SuperTed burst into the bathroom.

"Put on your waterproofs, Spotty!" he said. "We're going to rescue a stranded whale."

After only a few minutes, SuperTed and Spotty joined the girl on the beach. They stared at the huge creature in wonder. "Great Moons of Spot!" cried Spotty. "How did that get there?"

"It must have swum up to the beach and rolled in with the tide," said SuperTed. "If we don't drag it back out to sea, it'll die."

Firing their rockets at full power, SuperTed and Spotty picked up the whale's tailfin and heaved with all their might. The girl ran to the other end and pushed gently against the whale's head.

"Umph! Arff! Rumph!" They all groaned with the effort, and slowly the whale began to slide across the sand and rocks.

It slipped into the water and quickly dived beneath the waves.

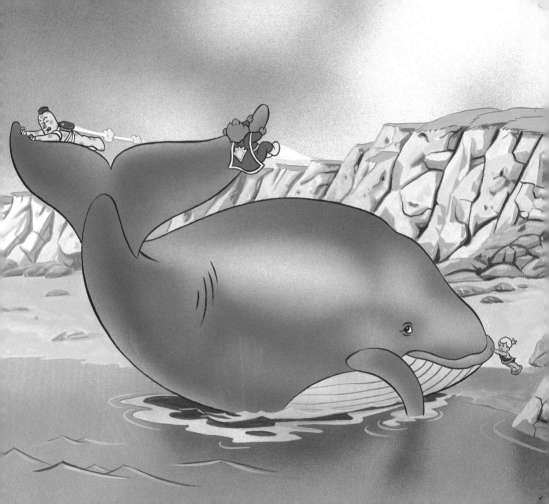

"Come on, Spotty!" said SuperTed, turning to his friend. "That whale stranded itself on purpose. It might need our help!"

Soon our two friends were swimming beneath the surface of the ocean, following the whale as it sailed over huge underwater cliffs and through reefs of multi-coloured corals. On their journey they passed the wreck of an old Spanish galleon, shimmering in a patch of sunlight beneath them.

They swam for miles and miles before the whale finally began to slow down. As SuperTed looked up, he could see two shapes floating listlessly near the surface.

They had reached their destination.

The whale had brought them to its family. As SuperTed and Spotty rose to the surface, a baby whale swam limply across their path. In its side was the broken end of a harpoon. The baby whale was obviously in great pain.

SuperTed grabbed the end of the harpoon and, as gently as possible, he pulled it free. The baby whale was very relieved and he and his parents shot to the surface and blew joyful spouts of air from their blowholes.

SuperTed and Spotty watched the whales disappear.

"Can I get back to my bath now, SuperTed?" asked Spotty.

"Not yet," replied SuperTed. "That harpoon came from a whaling ship. We'd better find it before any more whales are hurt!"

Then they rocketed into the air and flew out over the sea.

Not far away, a ship ploughed through the waves. In it were Texas Pete, Bulk and Skeleton, dressed in sou'westers and oilskins.

Tex peered into a small radar screen. "See those three dots? They're whales . . . heh, heh . . . great big blubbery blue whales. They won't get away from us this time. Hard to starboard!"

Bulk held the wheel and hesitated. Starboard? What did that mean? Why could not Tex say "right" or "left" like everyone else?

Eventually he closed his eyes and took his hands off the wheel.

It spun round like a catherine wheel, catching Skeleton under the chin and sending his head flying.

"Hey, Bulk!"

By now, SuperTed and Spotty were overhead.

"Look, SuperTed!" yelled Spotty. "Down there! It's a boat!"

They quickly changed course and flew down towards the whaling ship. Bulk was the first to see them. He stared into the sky and called out to Tex.

"Hey, I think I can see something in the sky . . . sort of hurtling towards us."

Tex leaped to the harpoon gun, which was already primed with explosive, and pointed it into the sky.

"I've got that sawn-off sack of stuffing in my sights," he chuckled. "I'll pepper his padding all across the sky!"

Then he fired the harpoon directly at SuperTed.

SuperTed dived out of the way, but the explosive point of the harpoon detonated behind him and blew him into Spotty's arms.

Below them, Tex yelled with glee, "Yipee-eye-oh . . . yeah! Bullseye!" Then he turned the harpoon back towards the sea.

The three whales broke the surface together, sending fountains of air and spray shooting out of their blowholes.

"There they blow, Tex!" shouted Skeleton.

Tex lined them up in the sight of his harpoon gun and fired. The harpoon shot towards the whales, its long rope whistling through the air behind it.

"Come on, SuperTed!" shouted Spotty. "You've got to do something!"

SuperTed was still dazed but, all the same, he struggled out of Spotty's arms and fired his rocket boots at full power. He was too late to catch the harpoon, but he tugged at the rope and sent it flying off course. Then he turned round and headed for the boat.

Tex started to shout, "Just wait till I've reloaded this harpoon. I'll tear you to tatters!"

Just then, the boat seemed to lift out of the water. One of the whales had turned back and surfaced directly underneath its hull. The whaling ship rose out of the water and broke apart with a loud crack.

SuperTed found himself face to face with Texas Pete.

Tex stood on the back of the whale and pointed the harpoon gun straight at his furry enemy.

"Don't move, SuperTed, or I'll blast you all the way back to your toyshop shelf!"

SuperTed looked around for Spotty. He needed help! Then, suddenly, there was a loud whistling sound, as the whale puffed a stream of air out of its blowhole. The column of air caught Tex by the seat of his pants and lifted him head over heels, but not before his hand had caught on the trigger of the harpoon gun.

Bulk and Skeleton were holding the rope and, as the harpoon shot across the sky, they were pulled up high above the ocean after it.

Later, SuperTed and Spotty watched as the whales swam away towards the horizon.

"Well done, SuperTed," said Spotty. "You saved the whales."

"Don't congratulate me, Spotty," SuperTed replied. "It was the big whale from the beach. It saved us all."

Books in the SuperTed series

SuperTed and the Pothole Rescue
SuperTed and the Blue Whales
SuperTed Kicks up the Dust
SuperTed and Tex's Magic Spell
SuperTed and Bulk's Story
SuperTed in SuperTed's Dream
SuperTed and the Lumberjacks
SuperTed and Mother Nature
SuperTed Meets Zappy and Zoppy
SuperTed and the Green Planet
SuperTed at the Bottom of the Sea
SuperTed and the Hungry Monkeys
SuperTed and the Crystal Ball
SuperTed and the Gun Smugglers
SuperTed in the Arctic